JENNY'S CORNER

JENNY'S

CORNER

FREDERIC BELL

Drawings by Zenowij Onyshkewych

Random House New York

All rights reserved under International and Pan-American Copyright Conventions. Published in the United States by Random House, Inc., New York, and simultaneously in Canada by Random House of Canada Limited, Toronto.

Library of Congress Cataloging in Publication Data.

Bell, Frederic. Jenny's corner.

SUMMARY: A little girl's love for deer results in a prohibition on hunting in her valley.
   [1. Hunting – Fiction] I. Onyshkewych, Zenowij, illus. II. Title. PZ7.B3889175Je   [Fic]   73-18741
ISBN 0-394-82741-4   ISBN 0-394-92741-9 (lib. bdg.)

Manufactured in the United States of America

Design by Grace Clarke

To Jenny,
who believed me.

JENNY'S CORNER

At the westernmost edge of New Jersey, just before the gentle farmlands of Hunterdon County slope downward toward the Delaware River, the traveler on the old High Road between Flemington and Frenchtown will catch his first glimpse of the hills of Pennsylvania. Ahead of him, seven or eight miles distant, and often shrouded in the mist that rises from the river, lie the foothills of the Kittatinnies. And although this story I am about to tell took place more than a hundred years ago, when the High Road was made of dust and the vehicle upon it was a Reston wagon drawn by a heavy-breathing team of four, no traveler from that day to this has failed to sense an ancient comfort in his soul when he first sees those welcoming hills of Pennsylvania.

And so it was with William Drury, who, in the spring of 1856, led his team down the High Road, and into Frenchtown, and across the Delaware into those hills that were to become home to his family. A hundred acres he had purchased, with a good stone house and barn, but a thousand acres to either side bear the name to this day of his daughter, Jenny Drury.

This is the story they tell of the Drurys, and of Jenny, and if you have the good fortune to find your way into these beautiful hills, then seek out the hamlet of Erwinna and turn inland on the old Headquarters Road. Within three miles you will come to Jenny's Corner, a cluster of homes beside the road with woods and fields rising to the north and south. These lands are tilled, harvested, and

4

forested—but never hunted. For in all these acres, not a man has fired a gun in more than a century. The Weavers will tell you, for their grandfathers, and some of their fathers, were here in 1856 when the Drurys came. Many nights around their huge Pennsylvania hearths the Weavers sat quietly as children and heard the tale of why this valley is called Jenny's Corner, and why, every fall since 1856, the Weaver men have left their work and protected the valley from hunters until the season is over.

Jenny was nine in that spring of
1856, the youngest of the four Drury girls, and
she had a deep and innocent fondness for things
that were wild and lonely, be it an animal, or a
tree, or a brooding sweep of land. There was a
sadness in her, and though she was by far the mer-
riest of her sisters in their company, she was often
happiest alone in her room where she would sit on
the wide sill of the window and gaze steadily at the
small pond and the field that lay to the south of

the house. It was here that the deer would come to drink and feed at dusk, a miracle that Jenny had never witnessed until she came to live in this Pennsylvania valley.

First the doe would come, emerging warily from the heavy pine woods that bordered one side of the pond. Heads up, their senses alert to every sound and shadow, they would stand for a moment at the edge of the water. Then, as silently as the mist gathering on the pond, the fawns would appear. Mottled brown and white, standing on unsteady legs spread wide for balance, they would lower their heads and drink with their mothers. In the next instant the deer would be gone, vanishing mysteriously before Jenny's eyes—beautiful, magic creatures that appeared and disappeared at the very moment of twilight. On certain nights when the wind was from the south, and if the dogs were still, and if no one slammed a door or raised his voice, scores of deer would file silently into the field beyond the pond, their moving forms visible in the soft afterlight of dusk. More than once the enchantment of the scene had worked its spell on Jenny and she had fallen asleep on the sill, only to be gently lifted into bed by her father when he checked on the oil lamps before retiring.

One May evening after supper, Mr. Drury took Jenny into a field that had just been sown with timothy seed. The wind was from the southwest, summery in feeling, and the man and his daughter stood for a moment, feeling the air and sensing the sweet rebirth of the land.

"We'll get our corn into the ground early this year," said Mr. Drury, "maybe twenty acres of it. We need warm nights for corn, Jenny, and this will be a year for warm nights. We'll plant it in that field you're always looking at south of the pond."

"Do deer eat corn, Father?"

He laughed. "Yes, Jenny, deer eat corn, sometimes too much of it. Unless there's a dog around at night, they'll come into a man's back-yard, ten feet from his door, and eat the corn he's growing for his own table. They eat plants and apples, even roots and bark when times are lean, but they'll walk ten miles to get at a man's corn. When the snow lies heavy in this valley, Jenny, and the men are working inside their barns and the fields are quiet, you'll see a lot of deer in our cornfield. They'll kick away at a drift to get at the scraps underneath, and sometimes you'll see them roll in the snow, trying to melt it."

On the way back to the house, Jenny asked if she could plant a special patch of corn for the deer. "It would be their own corn," she said, "and they wouldn't have to steal it."

"Good idea," said Mr. Drury, swinging his daughter onto his shoulders. "But instead of going to all that trouble, why don't I just plant an extra row in the cornfield. After we harvest it this fall, we'll store it in a special place in the corncrib and you can feed it to the deer this winter."

Jenny was immensely pleased. From her eagle's roost atop her father's shoulders she looked into the field where the corn was to be planted. And suddenly, in Jenny's eyes, it was winter, and there was snow on the ground, and dozens of hungry deer were silently standing in a circle. Within the circle stood a little red-haired girl with corn in her hand.

After the children had been put to bed that evening, William Drury and his wife sat outside on the edge of the stone porch. The peepers could be heard and the smell of earth was in the air. Except for the oil lamp glimmering faintly from the window behind them, not a light was to be seen. Peace and timelessness were upon the land, and the man was content. He had not moved to this valley lightly, and he had done so only when the land he farmed on the northern edge of Manhattan had been annexed by the city, requiring him to leave. His first thought had been to change his trade, but he wanted his children to be raised on the land and in accord with his own precepts. So he had traveled west from Manhattan and found this valley and bought this farm. And he was glad for having done it.

The land and the weather had been good

to him; the warmth of May had been felt in April and the spring rains had come early, softening the red, shaly soil for the plow. But there had been an even greater good fortune for William Drury, and now, as he sat on his porch feeling the valley around him, he thought of Jonas Weaver.

The Drurys had moved onto their farm in late March, and for three weeks, sometimes by sun and sometimes by moonlight, William Drury had worked himself to exhaustion taking care of those first things that had to be done. A roof had to be patched, a floor reboarded, a windlass rebuilt. These were essential matters, and among them was the replacing of a water line to the cistern in the barn. At the exact moment he was removing the heavy hand pump from the top of the cistern, he had met Jonas Weaver.

The man was a giant, filling the barn doorway from jamb to jamb and from top to bottom, fully blocking out the light and startling William Drury so badly that he dropped the pump and sprang back in fear.

"I didn't mean t' surprise ye," said the man, stepping back into the light. But what William Drury saw in that light was of scarce comfort to him. He was quite sure he had never laid eyes on a wilder, more fearsome form. My God, he thought to himself, the man must be seven feet tall!

If you've ever seen a fieldstone rubbed raw by wind and weather, cracked, peeled, and pitted, you've seen the face of William Drury's visitor. It was crowned by a bushel of black, tangled hair that fell below his shoulders and seemed to grow into, or out of, an immense bearskin jacket—and had that jacket been alive, it would not have surprised William Drury. If the man had been anywhere near the size of a normal human being, William Drury would have spoken a word of welcome, but there was no welcome in his heart for this strange monster. He waited wordlessly for whatever God or the Devil would do next.

"I be Jonas Weaver," said the visitor, lifting an arm the size of a young tree and pointing it in the direction of the large fields behind the barn. "Ye'll have t' plow come two weeks. I have fourteen sons, and I thought ye might like t' have some of 'em."

The voice broke the spell that had taken hold of William Drury, for the man's speech was touched with the flavor of ancient Britain and belonged to the valley folk he had met. Whoever this man was, he was a neighbor, for better or for worse, and despite his appearance there was good will in his voice.

"That's very good of you," said William Drury cautiously, struggling to get his tongue moving again. "But we have no money to pay for help this year. We thought we'd just set out those crops we could take care of ourselves."

"Well, I be bringin' th' boys over a week from Monday, an' if yer wife will take 'em a little water in th' fields now an' then, they be much obleeged to her."

"I can't accept charity, Mr. Weaver."

Jonas grunted and mounted his horse, a

Percheron showing the marks of heavy field work. He settled himself in the saddle and spoke:

"We all be takin' a little help now an' then, Mr. Drury. It ain't charity. Ye might sled us over some shale come winter when th' roads freeze. We be buildin' a dam an' don't have shale t' where we live."

And without another word between them, Jonas Weaver was gone, cantering across the fields toward a distant stand of hardwood. That must be where he lives, thought William Drury, in the woods, perhaps, or maybe beyond, near the river. It would be a fitting place for a man of such wildness.

But there was nothing of wildness in the offer that Jonas Weaver had brought. In fact, if William Drury were to ask his Maker for a favor during this first spring on the farm, it would be for exactly what Jonas had offered him—the help of strong, willing men in the fields, so that he might feed his family well during a first winter in a strange country. William Drury had judged Jonas

14

by his appearance, and this troubled him. "We'll see," he said to himself, as he again started to struggle with the hand pump. "We'll see who this Jonas Weaver is. God knows, his looks could scare a grown man half to death."

Jonas Weaver was good to his word.

On the promised Monday, an hour after dawn, he arrived with three of his sons, an ox, a Percheron, and a wagonload of plows, parts, and tools. Within an hour, the first field was under plow, and within three hours, Jonas and William Drury had walked off sixty-five acres, discussing and deciding which crops would be best suited for each field, the amount of seed that should be bought, and where it should be bought. By the end of that first day, Jonas Weaver was a friend and brother to William Drury.

It took fourteen days to plow, harrow, and plant, the three Weaver boys doing the work of any ten William Drury had ever known. On one morning, when there was a threat of rain in the air,

Jonas walked to the highest point of the field to be worked that day and looked carefully at the low, grey sky, his huge frame silhouetted against the horizon like an old gnarled oak. He raised his arms high over his head, aiming them at the fast-moving scud clouds. When he returned, William Drury said, "You looked like an old devil up there, scaring the rain out of the sky."

The old man laughed. "I be no devil, William. But I be a mite touchy on th' arms about th' weather. If th' hair stands up, it be a day or two of rain. If it lay flat, it be nothin' more than maybe a shower. It be flat today, so we be plowin'."

When the work of the Weavers was finished . . . when the fields lay planted and baking in the strong spring sun, a miracle at least a year ahead of its time, the Weaver boys loaded their wagon and came to the house to thank Mrs. Drury. She had brought them water several times a day, and had provided them with baskets of bread and kettles of stew—a daily larder so bountiful that had the boys eaten a third of it they would have been unable to lift a rein or walk a hundred yards. Jonas stood awkwardly beside his horse, hoping his sons would find the words to say the right things. William Drury walked over to him and had considerable trouble finding his own words of gratitude.

He looked up into that craggy face he'd come to respect so much, and said, "You've done a fine thing for us, Jonas."

"Ye be set now fer spring," said Jonas uncomfortably, quickly mounting his horse. "Ye can set out th' corn yerself when th' weather warms enough, an' we be comin' back fer th' harvest work."

"Jonas, you can count on all the shale you can use this winter, I promise you that. But it's small payment for all you've done. Are you sure there's no more I can offer?"

"Well, there is one thing," said Jonas. "We been huntin' these lands of yours since I were in th' cradle. We eat what we shoot. Would ye be allowin' us t' hunt fer deer this fall?"

"Certainly," said William Drury instantly.

"This land is yours to hunt as you please."

"Thank ye," said Jonas.

So it was not just the goodness of the land and the weather that William Drury was thinking about on that warm May night when he sat on his porch. He was thinking, too, of the goodness of the Weavers and of the fields that were now planted and growing. He turned to his wife, who sat beside him, and said gently, "Hannah, we are very much blessed."

In a short while, they went into the house, took the oil lamp from the window, and quietly ascended the stairs. As was his nightly custom, and his last act of each day, William Drury checked the lamp in his youngest daughter's room. There, for the second time in a week, he found Jenny asleep on the sill.

He picked her up gently and put her into bed.

Summer, for Jenny Drury, when the fields shimmered in the heat and the pond grew low, when the valley men were in their fields being broiled alive over the brick-hard earth as they went about their weeding and cultivating from dawn till long after dusk—summer was none of this for Jenny. It was a time of walking in the cool pine woods and discovering the nesting places of deer in the pine needles and wild grass . . . of following deer trails to a still-running spring, delicately alive,

19

hidden on the edge of a land of brown grass and blazing sun. Jenny's chores were to feed the domestic animals, and this she finished regularly before ten in the morning. And then the fields and the valley were hers.

Sometimes she would pack a small lunch and wander deep into the pine woods. There was no fear in her of such things. Endless, marching rows of pine and spruce, their lower trunks spiked with dried and dead limbs . . . faint, faraway specks of sun and sky through shadowy arches of immense green boughs . . . this was the home of the doe and the fawn, and this was home and comfort to Jenny. Spreading her neckerchief over the wild grass, she would eat her lunch in a suitable clearing, perhaps only a few yards wide. Sometimes she would sit there quietly until late afternoon, hoping the deer would join her. Once she brought a small cake she had baked, and she left it in the clearing for the deer. The next morning she returned, and to her great delight she found the cake gone, the prints of deer everywhere in evidence. Never again did she fail to leave something for the deer.

Several times during that summer, the Weaver men saw Jenny Drury in the fields and woods far from home, and once Jonas himself, coming upon her in a distant field, raised her up to his huge saddle and took her home with a stern word of warning. William Drury spoke to his daughter about this, and though he did not restrict her to the farm property, he cautioned her against such far-ranging walks.

"Not that there is anything to be afraid of in the woods during the summer," he told her, "but if you should fall and hurt yourself, or become lost, how would we find you?"

Jenny understood, and although she continued to follow the fresh tracks of deer beyond the sight and sounds of the farm, she was more conscious of her obligations, and not again during that summer was she seen by the Weavers or any other neighbor.

She would sit on her sill in the evenings, never tiring of the beautiful creatures that came to see her at twilight. And she returned their visits during the days. This was summer for Jenny Drury.

Summer passed, and with it the growing of the crops, of which the most important to Jenny was the corn. She helped her father plant it in June, in the early morning, walking ten paces behind him and placing each seed herself in the shallow furrow left by the plow. Then her father reversed the plow and she watched as the soft earth was rolled and tumbled into the furrow, covering the seeds. At each end of the special row that was to be harvested for the deer, she placed a stone marker, and every morning thereafter on her way to the woods she would bend close to the ground and sight along the two markers to see if the corn had sprouted. The first shoots appeared in two weeks, green and tender, barely topping the warm earth, and when Jenny discovered them she immediately ran to the pine woods and spoke aloud into the silence: "The corn is growing. It's for you. Please don't eat it now."

Every day Jenny would speak to the deer, asking them to wait for winter and cautioning them against impatience.

In September the Weavers returned, twelve of them including Jonas, and it was a time of excitement and fulfillment. Huge, open-sided farm wagons were pulled into the ripe fields, and sweating, shirtless men seemed to swim in the golden wheat and grass, their sickles and ancient hand tools sparkling in the sun. In the evenings the Weavers did not immediately return home, as they had before, but came in from the fields and joined the Drurys at a long plank table that had been set up in the orchard near the house. Each afternoon Mrs. Drury and two of the Weaver women, helped by the four Drury girls, baked, boiled, scraped, shelled, fried, and served bushels of steaming food that bent the table under its weight, yet disappeared instantly.

"Serve it t' 'em in buckets!" Jonas bellowed once, when two of his sons were threatening each other's lives over a bowl of sweet potatoes. "Did man or God ever see sich a thing! Ye be better suited t' bein' harnessed t' th' wagons, 'stead of fillin' 'em!" He gave his sons a look that would have toppled a tree, and had their ears been longer they would have lain back against their heads in sheer fright. Then Jonas turned to Mrs. Drury, the slightest twinkle in his eyes. "I ask yer fergiveness fer these oxen, Mrs. Drury. I be sure they was tied t' th' stanchions in th' barn, but I see I was wrong."

Oh, the harvest was a time of high merriment for Jenny and the girls! When the food had been consumed, Jonas would order one of his sons to fetch the German squeeze-box they'd brought along, and as soon as Jonas had his barrel-like hands on it he'd strike a fast jig. The other men clapped their hands in time to the squeaks and strains and urged the women, particularly the Drury girls, to raise their skirts a bit and dance. Little Jenny was always the first to oblige, to the mortification of her sisters, and giggling under her mop of red hair she shamelessly performed pirou-

ettes and curtsies while her sisters gradually worked
their way onto the dance floor by fits and jerks.

When the shadows lengthened sufficiently,
leaving perhaps a half-hour of daylight, Jonas
would play his final chords and rise, saying his
good-bys as civilly as he knew how. He and the two
Weaver women would take their places on the seat
of the largest wagon, while the boys sprawled over
the tailgate or hung over the sides waving at the
Drury girls. Then off they'd go, merrily rolling
their way down the lane toward the road. Each
night, the Drurys would see them out of sight and
then go to bed in sheer, happy exhaustion.

The harvest was finished in a week, the
barn bulging to the roof with the good deeds of the
Weavers, and a degree of normalcy returned to the
Drury household.

For Jenny, the nearness of winter was now
the main concern. It didn't usually come early to
this valley; the long, cool days of autumn could be
expected to continue well into November without

a hint of snow. But this year there were snow flurries in mid-October, and by the first week in November there was an inch or two of snow covering the fields.

Jenny's corn had been harvested by the Weavers in September. It had been clearly marked by her father and stored away safely in the corncrib. But kernels and bits of broken cobs had fallen on the ground, and at least once each day since the harvest Jenny had gone to the cornfield to find what she could and take it back with her to the house for safekeeping. Even in November, Jenny was meticulous in retrieving every scrap she saw; heavier snows were sure to fall, when the deer would have a greater need for the corn.

Late one afternoon, with a strong northerly wind blowing that was certain to shift the snow around and lay the ground bare in spots, Jenny walked to the cornfield carrying a large basket. She had just reached the edge of the field when she heard a rifle shot. In the next instant a doe ran past her, coming so close she was sprayed with snow.

26

There was an acrid odor in the air, faintly sicken-
ing, the smell of fear given off by a frantic animal,
and Jenny understood. Her father was not a hunter, but he had shot a lame horse on their first farm,
and Jenny, who had been told to remain in the
house, had not obeyed. She had turned the corner
of the barn just as Mr. Drury pulled the trigger,
and she had seen the sudden spurt of blood and
watched the horse go down. She had smelled the
terror of the animal as it tried to raise its head a
final time, and she had seen the tears in her
father's eyes.

So Jenny knew the meaning of the rifle shot
as she stood on the edge of that frozen field.

The horror of it crept over her and she
screamed, "Stop it! Stop it! Don't shoot my deer!
Please! . . . Don't shoot my deer!"

But what was the child's voice against that
northern wind? And who would have obeyed it
had he heard it? Jenny dropped her basket and ran,
in utter panic, toward the house and her father. He
heard her screaming and ran to meet her, and he

swept her up into his arms.

"What is it, Jenny? Lord, what is it?"

"The deer . . . they're killing my deer," and she sobbed uncontrollably against her father's shoulder, hiding herself from a reality she could not have dreamed of in the most horrible of nightmares.

William Drury carried his daughter into the house. She was now as mute and unmoving as a stone.

"What is it, William?" asked Hannah, who had not heard the child's screams and was startled to see Jenny in her father's arms. "Is she hurt?" and she inspected Jenny from head to toe in a second.

"Yes," said William Drury, gently placing Jenny in the large chair by the fireplace, "but not in body. I should have known to tell her about the hunting. She is afraid for the deer. I will have to talk with her." William Drury had been foolish, and the moment had arrived for him to reckon with it. He knew full well of his daughter's love for the deer. He had not been sensible enough to tell her that they were food and clothing to the men of this valley and that their season had come.

"You should tell her now," said Hannah quietly. "This is not a thing to put off. I swear, she will neither eat nor sleep until all of this is explained."

"I know," he said, walking slowly to the hearth. He turned and faced Jenny, so fragile and far below him in the chair.

"Jenny," he said quietly, "do you hear me?"

"Yes," said Jenny, her face empty of expression.

So William Drury told her, as reasonably as he could and with as much understanding as lay within him, of the need for men to kill so that they might eat and clothe themselves, and that the death of the deer was not a waste, but a good thing for a dozen families in the valley.

"Jenny, Jenny . . . they will only take what they must. No more than that."

It was done. William Drury turned away, fearful of the hurt and disbelief he had seen in his child's eyes.

"I'll take her to her room now," said Hannah. "Perhaps later we'll bring her some milk."

And she took Jenny's hand and led her up the stairs.

There was no solace for Jenny in her father's words. In a moment of sound and horror, the pleasant world of Jenny Drury had become cold and hostile. Although she continued to search the field for her corn, digging for those kernels which had not yet been eaten by the deer or rotted under the wetness of the snow, there was no joy in it for her, nor hope. Each day, now, from her window, she could see the armed men come from the woods near the road and spread out along the far edge of the cornfield. In a slow death march, they would cross the field and enter the pines, flushing everything before them. Shots would ring out, and later the men would reappear, walking back across the field. She could hear their laughter and loud talk and see the bundles of steaming hides and meat flung across their shoulders or dragged behind them on skid poles. Jenny would watch in numbness, there being no more emotion left within her, except for those moments just before she fell asleep when relief would come as she wept for her deer. The corn she had gathered in baskets for safekeeping still stood in a corner of her room, bearing testimony to the broken world of Jenny Drury.

There are no official records, but there are some Weavers who remember being told it was November 27, 1856. Perhaps they are right, for never in the history of eastern Pennsylvania has there been a storm of wind, snow, and ice such as that which descended on the valley in that November; and many a man, sealed into his house by twenty-foot drifts that buried trees as though they were clumps of grass, must have taken his calendar and circled that date in awe. So the day was known for many years.

It was on the afternoon of that day, just before the storm began, when the sky was clear overhead but towering into a grey, granitelike cliff to the west, that one of Jonas' sons, Micah, shot and wounded a doe in the cornfield. The doe fell in the loose snow, rolled over, and regained its legs in an instant, and Jenny witnessed all of this from her window. She saw blood on the snow and she watched the doe move away, limping, toward the shelter of the low woods to the east.

No men who hunt as the Weavers hunt would have failed to track a wounded prey, though it meant crossing the river and following the animal halfway across New Jersey. They killed to eat, not for sport, and they wished no pain or hardship to the creatures that provided them with so much. But this doe, though limping, moved off at a steady pace no man could equal, and the experienced eye of Micah told him that the building storm would be upon them both in an hour, long before he could reach her.

So Micah did not follow the doe. He knew the doe would run to the east, ahead of the storm, and he knew every creek and ravine and hiding place she might be in when she stopped her flight and sought shelter. Micah decided he would seek her in the morning with the help of his brothers.

But not so Jenny.

The moment she saw the blood on the snow, she jumped from the sill with a cry and ran downstairs and out the door, unseen by anyone. Crying, driven by compassion for the wounded doe, she found the trail of blood leading across the field and along the hedgerow. She followed it, running at first, and then, as the trail grew fainter, slowing to a walk so as not to miss the grisly signs of passage. Micah did not see Jenny, for as soon as he had made up his mind not to track the doe that day, he had turned and hurried toward home.

The snow fell within the hour, and it came in sudden, heavy sheets of blinding white. The first gusts bent hedgerow cedars to the ground, and within minutes every trail left by human or animal was wiped from the earth. The Blizzard of '56 was upon the valley, and it bore down savagely on the wounded doe and the little red-haired girl.

That night, for William Drury, was not to be remembered for the storm alone. If Hell itself had descended on the valley, it would have made no impression on the man. When he returned from Erwinna that evening and found his wife and daughters nearly panic-stricken—for the women knew by then that Jenny was lost—he threw a blanket and reins on the youngest field horse he owned and strained the animal nearly to death in a dead run across the fields and through the woods to Jonas' farm.

He threw open the door to the old man's house and stood there, the howling of the wind and the blackness behind him, and screamed at Jonas:

"For God's sake, help us! Jenny is lost! She's in the woods!"

Even Jonas, who had no fear of anything alive, was startled at the terror in the man's voice.

He rose immediately and grabbed William Drury, pushing him down into a chair at the huge round table where the family was eating.

"Quiet, man!" he commanded. "Ye be in panic! Did ye say Jenny be lost in this storm?"

The sight of the Weaver men—seven or eight of them in that rough-hewn, soot-blackened room, smelling of sweat and leather and wildness—gave William Drury a moment of hope, and with all his mind he controlled himself enough to speak evenly.

"Jonas, Jenny is in the woods. She has no coat. She may be on my farm or off it, I don't know, but the women say she is not in any of the buildings or within a hundred yards of the house."

"When did she be gone?" asked Jonas, and in the same breath he ordered his wife to fill, immediately, a lantern for every man in the room.

"Before the storm hit. Hannah searched before the first snow fell. I was in Erwinna and didn't know."

"How long afore th' storm, Mr. Drury?"

It was Micah, and he had risen from his chair with intense interest.

"I don't know. Maybe an hour."

"I shot a doe on yer farm an hour afore th' storm. I let 'er run, thinkin' t' track 'er in th' mornin'. She be fast an' no sense trackin' 'er this night."

"What field did you shoot her in?" asked William Drury. He scarcely had need to ask, for he knew instantly and with a fearful certainty what the answer would be, and what Jenny had done. "Was it the cornfield?"

"Yes," said Micah. "She tumbled, an' then she moved off toward Cafferty Road."

"Then Jenny saw it," said William Drury, rising quickly from the table. "She saw it from the window and trailed it."

Jonas turned toward Micah and looked at him narrowly. "Can we be findin' that doe, Micah? She had up t' an hour t' travel an' then she'd a lay down. In forty years, I never seen a wounded deer cross a road, so she be t' th' west of Cafferty and t' th' north of Headquarters. There be six hundred acres or more in there, Micah. Can ye find 'er?"

"I be findin' 'er if any man alive find 'er," said Micah steadily, "an' it be best we stop talkin' an' start lookin'."

"I think she be in th' Frankenfield valley," said Jonas carefully. "There be th' deep creek in there an' th' woods be th' heaviest about. William an' me will search from here t' th' Frankenfield place. We be walkin' toward William's farm all th' while. Th' rest of ye go in twos . . . two along th' creek from Cafferty t' William's farm . . . two of ye follow th' ravine down from th' north toward Frankenfield . . . an' two of ye go in them pines between here an' William's." Then Jonas turned to William Drury, and with as much understanding and compassion as he could convey, he said, "William, she be in there, an' there be no rest fer us this night 'til we find 'er."

Not another word was spoken as the men dressed hurriedly. For five generations, Weaver men had hunted these woods and passed along what they learned to their sons, and each man in the room was searching his soul for every scrap of knowledge that could help him find Jenny Drury.

The lanterns were distributed, and in a moment the men had stepped into that raging world of storm. Jonas and William set off at a fast pace toward the slope of land that led into the wild Frankenfield valley.

"It not be too cold," said Jonas as they struck the rocky base of the valley. "If she be in here, she be alive." He pointed ahead into the darkness, his finger following the outline of a small, fast-running stream. "Micah an' one of th' other boys be comin' down from there, an' we be goin' up. It be a mile or more of hard walkin' on stone an' in th' water, but this be th' most likely place t' my thinkin'. Ye walk on th' left side of th' creek, just so ye can still see my lantern, an' I be walkin' on th' right th' same way. Don't expect t' see th' girl or th' deer. Look fer a clump of white. Use yer eyes."

William Drury did not have to be told

more. He sprang across the stream, taking his position a hundred feet to the side of it, and walked forward into the swirling snow. He couldn't see fifty yards ahead of him, and although he called out for Jenny with every step, he knew his voice could not be heard over the howling of the wind in the tops of the trees. Panic boiled within him. Nothing, he thought, could be more hopeless. In all creation there was no place as unforgiving and hostile as this deathly little valley of jutting rocks and hellish blackness, and the vision of Jenny huddled against a tree or a rock, covered with snow, the lifeblood being frozen out of her, nearly drove him mad.

He had stopped to adjust the wick in his lantern, his fingers fumbling with impatience, when the sound of Jonas' voice came to him dimly through the heaviness of the snow. He had to cup his ears to be sure he had heard it.

"Here, William! Here! I've found 'er! It's Jenny!"

In one headlong rush, William Drury

threw himself across the creek toward the faint circle of lamplight and fell on his knees before the little bundle of snow and cloth that was his daughter.

"She be alive, William. She be breathin' an' there still be warmth in 'er. See fer yerself."

William Drury saw for himself. And he cried unashamedly, and tore off his coat and wrapped Jenny in it and lifted her into his arms. Then they walked to the Drury farm, the huge woodsman clearing the way through the broken limbs and brush so that no further harm would come to Jenny Drury that night.

For two days and nights the storm
continued. When it finally ceased, its dark edges
still to be seen to the east and the cold, clear winds
driving in hard from the west, the snow lay in
huge drifts across the fields, like immense, mo-
tionless waves. It would be weeks before the roads
could be rolled and packed for the sleds, and no
horse born could have walked a mile in that deep,
white wilderness. There was no movement in the
valley except by those on snowshoes, and in this

manner William Drury walked to the home of Jonas Weaver with a request as hopeless as asking for the snow to melt in an hour.

Jenny Drury lay dying. It was not because of the exposure she had suffered during the storm, for that had harmed her little. It was because of despair. Her love and compassion for the deer were too much for her to bear in a world of hunting and killing. The bloodied trail of the crippled doe had overwhelmed her with grief, destroying what scant hope she still had left for the deer, and the child wanted to die. Death was indeed coming to her as she wished, and William Drury knew that the only human who could defeat it was Jonas Weaver. For the second time in less than a week, William Drury faced that old man and his sons in search of Jenny's life.

For half an hour, William Drury spoke to the woodsmen about his daughter's love for the deer and her terror of the hunting . . . spoke to rough, hard men who were raised from birth with a musket or rifle in their hands, and to whom the killing of a deer for meat was as natural as digging up a potato or a turnip. They harvested deer as they harvested their crops, and even at this moment, as William Drury talked, they and their children were eating the fruits of their hunting skills—good red venison that kept them alive in times such as this. There was little hope in William Drury that such men would do as he asked. If he were simply asking them not to hunt on the Drury farm, his request would be granted immediately. But Jenny had said much in her delirium, and the broken words had shown William Drury what must be done if she were to regain hope and life. What he had to ask of these Weaver men was that they hunt no more in the valley.

No one spoke when William Drury finished. The whine of the wind and the crackling of the cedar logs on the hearth were the only sounds in the great, bare room. The men had willingly risked their lives for Jenny during the storm, and they were touched by the words of William Drury. But the man's request went beyond reason.

"William," said Jonas softly, leaning forward on the table, "what ye ask be not ours t' give. This valley be not ours. There's th' Frankenfield place where we found th' young 'un. An' there be two other farms in there aside from yours an' ours. There be over two thousand acres in th' valley, William. My God, man, ye cannot ask us t' go around it, or over it, t' hunt our meat. We not be huntin' on yer farm no more, an' th' little girl be gettin' over it. Ye wait an' see."

"She won't get over it, Jonas," said William Drury. "Now, Jonas, you told me yourself once that the widow who owns the lands to the west of my farm has never accepted a piece of venison from you, although you've stocked your table a hundred times from her woods."

"That be true," said Jonas.

"All right," said William Drury. "So the widow wouldn't mind if nobody hunted her land; as a matter of fact, she'd probably be happy about it. One of the other farms you speak of is only thirty acres, and every foot of it lies along Headquarters Road where you'd never hunt anyway. That leaves only Frankenfield. He's an old man, nearly eighty I hear, and I would be more than willing to supply him with all the beef and pork he can eat."

"No, it don't!" said Jonas quickly, rising from the table. "No it don't only leave Frankenfield. It leaves me an' my sons an' twelve hundred acres among us!" Jonas was furious. "William," he said roughly, "ye be hurtin' fer yer daughter, an' I be understandin' that, an' there ain't a man in this room wouldn't give his life fer 'er. But not th' lives of our own children! What ye ask is not t' be. We be stayin' off yer land, an' we be huntin' no nearer t' it than we must. But that be final!"

Jonas sat down heavily. He had not meant to be so angry with his friend, but he could no more conceive of ordering his sons not to hunt in the valley than he could see himself selling his soul to the Devil—and both notions seemed about the same to him. God put the deer here, and they gave his family food and clothing. It wasn't right for a man to turn his back on such God-given bounty. William Drury was a friend, and he was in torment, but he was a fool to ask such a thing. There was no doubt in Jonas' mind that Jenny would recover if he simply stopped his sons from hunting on the Drurys' farm, and he had no intention of thinking any more about it. His life was a rough, practical existence with no room or occasion for self-doubt. It was exactly this nature that enabled him to find Jenny in the storm when her father would have been totally incapable of it. Few men would have been incautious enough to argue anything at all with Jonas Weaver, and had William Drury not come for the good reason he had, for the sake of his daughter, his safety would have been seriously in question.

Micah rose from the table, putting a hand on his father's shoulder, and he spoke quietly to William Drury. There was understanding in his voice, and perhaps even kindness. "Mr. Drury, I think it be best if ye go home t' yer daughter now. We feel pain fer ye . . . all of us do, an' we can understan' yer feelin's. I pray that Jenny lives, an' as fer me, I would give up th' huntin' t' save 'er. Jonas didn't mean what he be soundin' like, but ye asked a hard thing of 'im, ye know."

William Drury stood up. There was no fear in him of Jonas or of any Weaver in the room. For a moment, blanketed by frustration and a deep anger of his own—overwhelmed by a sense of failure—he wanted to reach for a rifle he saw leaning against a chair and coldly and systematically destroy every man in the room. It was a controlled, clear thought by an intelligent man who had been pushed to the edge.

Abruptly, William Drury turned and walked out the door. He laced his snowshoes to his feet and set off at a fast pace toward home. He had made up his mind to tell Jenny that the Weavers had agreed to his request . . . that the hunting would be stopped and there would be no more killing of the deer throughout the entire valley. This news would be the immediate hope Jenny needed, and, with God's help, it would bring her back to health. As for next year, when the hunting season came again, he would fulfill his words to Jenny by any means required. He understood what this might demand of him, but Jenny was not to die as long as William Drury could prevent it. The problems he might face next year with the Weavers were utterly unimportant compared with saving his child's life now.

When he arrived home, he called for Hannah and told her what had happened at the Weavers and of the decision he had made. Fear showed plainly in Hannah's face, but the child's life was in the balance and she had no choice but to agree. They decided to tell Jenny immediately.

Jonas was old, but his legs were long and he had the strength of a horse in them. He left his house ten minutes after William Drury went out the door in anger. He left without a word to his sons, simply rising from the table, donning his coat and snowshoes, and striking out hard and fast on the clear trail of William Drury. So fast did

Jonas travel that he crossed the snow-covered boundaries of the Drury farm and came halfway to the barn before William Drury reached his own door, unaware that Jonas was following him. Jonas paused for a moment in the yard, looking up at the windows of the room he knew to be Jenny's. Then, swiftly, he unlaced his snowshoes and walked across the porch to the door. He didn't knock, but pushed the door aside roughly, his big hands barely managing to turn the doorknob, saving the door and sash from total destruction.

"Where be Jenny?" he shouted at the startled Drurys. They had just that moment started for Jenny's room, and there was scarcely any wish on their part to see Jonas. William stared at the man intently . . . there could only be one reason Jonas would come to the house at this time and ask for Jenny. Slowly, trying to be certain of Jonas' motives, William Drury felt the beginning of a miracle.

"I'll have time fer ye later," said Jonas impatiently. "Fer now, take me t' yer daughter."

"Follow us," said William, and the three of them climbed the stairs to Jenny's room, where Jonas had to bend forward to keep his head from knocking holes in the beams. Below him, huddled in a corner of her bed, lay Jenny Drury, pale as the sheet she lay on and half her weight of a week ago.

"Jenny," said Jonas softly, and there were tears in his eyes, for he had not dreamed of the emotion he would feel upon seeing this child he had so lately rescued from death and who was so clearly at the door of it now.

"Jenny, can ye hear me? It be Jonas Weaver, Jenny."

Jenny opened her eyes and saw him dimly.

"Hello, Mr. Weaver," she said softly.

"Jenny, I have good news fer ye. Never agin will me or my boys hunt fer deer in this valley. Do ye hear me, Jenny? All th' way from Erwinna t' th' covered bridge . . . even in that field where I found ye this summer . . . there will never be huntin' in this valley agin. All th' deer be yours,

Jenny. Do ye hear me, child?"

If an angel had appeared at the window of that little room and come to Jenny's bed and spoken what Jonas had spoken, no greater joy could have shone in Jenny Drury's eyes, and no serum could have brought more promise of life. What Jonas saw from his watered eyes at that moment was the resurrection of a child. He bent as close to her as the furniture would allow. "Jenny," he said, "I give ye th' word of Jonas Weaver that what I say t' ye will be done. There be no more huntin' in this valley, now or ever. This I swear t' ye, Jenny Drury."

The child reached out for him and touched his sleeve, and then, crying with happiness, she fell back into a deep sleep.

Nothing was said between Jonas and the Drurys as they descended the stairs. Both the Drurys were too overcome to speak. But Jonas had a word reserved for William Drury, and when they reached the porch door, he spoke firmly.

"It was yer anger that moved me as fast as I come. I would 'ave come, William, but not fer maybe an hour or two. Micah saw it in yer eyes, an' said ye might 'ave tried t' use th' rifle on us. Ye be a fool, William. Ye would 'ave died in an instant. But yer anger was enough, an' it moved me, fer ye would 'ave told th' child a lie I 'spect, an' she would not 'ave believed ye, an' she would not 'ave believed me, neither, when I come later."

William Drury stood as though numbed. Gripped by fear and agony for a week, he struggled to grasp the sudden, liberating miracle that had just occurred in the room above his head.

"I be angry when ye spoke t' me about th' huntin', an' I tell ye that God, Himself, will not judge me harsh fer that anger, fer ye were takin' th' food an' clothin' from us, an' ye should give a man a minute or two afore ye 'spect 'im t' shake yer hand an' agree wi' ye. Yer little girl lay dyin', an' ye thought ye would get no help from us. Now ye 'ave it, William, an' when my boys get frostbit climbin' them hills t' th' north of this valley, an' when they fall in t' creeks they ain't never seen afore, I'll be sendin' 'em over here fer warmth an' food an' comfort. Ye judge an old, ugly man too harsh, William. We be friends ferever if ye get some sense. God bless th' both of ye an' little Jenny."

Jonas opened the door and stepped out onto the porch, breathing deeply of the frigid air, like a horse led out of a cramped stall. William Drury followed him, took the old man's hand, and said, simply, "Thank you."

As Jonas laced on his snowshoes, Hannah bent and kissed him on the cheek. Jonas mumbled something, pulled his collar tightly around his neck, and then plowed his way in the direction of the barn. In a few moments, the huge figure of Jonas Weaver, wilder and hardier than any the storm had tossed upon that frozen landscape, passed from view over the white crest of the hayfield.

Jonas lived for twenty years after making his vow to Jenny, and not once during those twenty years did a man raise a gun in the valley for fear of being dragged by his neck to the feet of that awesome Weaver. During deer season, two or three of Jonas' sons would go off to the north to hunt while the rest of them patrolled the valley on horseback. In the early mornings they would meet at the point where Cafferty Road comes up from the south and joins Headquarters Road, and from there they would spread out into the valley. That crossroads became known as "Jenny's Corner," and it was here that Jonas himself took his post, stopping all travelers at the intersection and inquiring about their intentions. If they were hunters, he would say, "There be good huntin' t' th' north an' south of this valley, an' I be wishin' ye luck, but this here be Jenny's Corner, an' ye are not t' go left nor right wi' yer rifles."

There were some unfortunate strangers who ignored Jonas' warning, went back along the road to a suitable spot, and then walked cross-country to reach the valley. None of these men, after having gone a hundred yards into the valley, failed to meet up with the mounted Weavers, either in the fields or in the woods; and no man who met with them had any further fear of Armageddon or Hell, for the warning he was given by these hard, quiet woodsmen would freeze the blood in his body. He would tell others to beware of the Weavers and Jenny's Corner, and in a remarkably short time it was a rare hunter in eastern Pennsylvania who did

56

not have a particular valley marked very clearly on his map.

Jenny Drury was at Jonas' bedside when he died, and when he commanded his son Micah to keep the pledge that had been made to Jenny. Micah kept the vow, setting as firm a hand on the valley as Jonas had. And Micah's sons, and now their sons, have continued to honor the promise made by Jonas Weaver when he kneeled at the side of a dying child.

As for Jenny, she married and raised a family on the farm, eventually planting all of the tillable acres in corn, except for a small plot which she used for her family's table vegetables. After the corn was harvested each fall, it was stored and then set out on the frozen fields in winter for the deer. Up to the day she died, which was not until after the turn of the century, Jenny Drury walked the fields and woods of that lovely valley, caring for the animals she loved so deeply. She was buried on the farm, on a hill that overlooked the house and pine woods. And although this may seem more legend than truth, it was solemn Micah, an old man by then, who said that a doe and her fawn came out of the woods as the last spadeful of earth was placed on Jenny Drury's grave, and, "payin' no mind t' th' people, th' doe lay down atop th' grave, her fawn wi' 'er. There be grown men who cried, an' I be among 'em."

There are Weavers who work the fields today within sight of the Drurys' house. It stands now as it did then, its thick walls of Pennsylvania fieldstone impervious to time and weather. All is the same . . . the pond, the open field where the doe was wounded, the immense barn with its weathered red siding. Even the pine woods, hardly a foot taller than in Jenny's time, still crowd to the edge of the pond as if waiting for a little red-haired girl to appear with her basket and neckerchief.